To Evelyn,
Merry Christmas, 20.
Love, A-Pops & Mumsie

MW00951731

Yes, Grandma a LADYBUG went to Bethlehem

Elaine M. Hameister

"Ladybugs are lucky"

illustrated by
Bonnie Lemaire

Elaine Hameister
2008

Copyright © 2007 Elaine M. Hameister

All rights reserved.

ISBN: 1-4196-8450-7

ISBN-13: 978-1419684500

Visit www.booksurge.com to order additional copies.

To my dear friend Jan, the
Grandmother of two-year old Addison,
who announced she would be a ladybug in
The Sunday School Christmas Pageant.

Upon hearing that, Grandma e-mailed me with the question:
"Was there a LADYBUG at the Nativity?"

This little book is my answer.

"GOD made everything that creepeth on earth". That's what it says in the Bible in the first book called Genesis, verses 24 and 25. The Bible goes on to list all the creepy crawlers: locusts, ants, grasshoppers, bees, caterpillars, cankerworms, fleas, maggots, flies, and lice. Yikes!

Can you find a bee?

A long, long time ago God made a perfect garden called Eden, and no garden is perfect without ladybugs. Some things are imperfect, like people, and the first mention of a ladybug in the Bible is in that same book of Genesis, when God says to Eve, "Lady, you bug me." *But that's another story.*

Ladybugs protected all kinds of things, even very big creatures, from being harmed by bad bugs. The little red bugs were like flares, and frightened the bad black bugs away.

Can you find 3 creatures?

God told Noah to build a wooden ark because a great flood would come. Noah knew he had to protect the ark against termites, because termites would eat the wood and destroy the ark. So, he called a family of ladybugs to guard the gangplank. Even though the termites taunted the little ladies , singing, "Ladybug, ladybug, fly away home, your house is on fire"------the ladybugs stood guard. *And that's another story, too.*

Can you find a ladybug?

Itty Bitty Addy was the tiniest of ladybugs, and she searched for beautiful gardens to protect. She loved the desert flowers, but in the winter, nighttime in the desert was very cold for Itty Bitty Addy. One winter evening the sky was very dark, but a bright star shone. Addy shivered. She flew around the sky as fast as she could, trying to keep warm, but still she shivered.

And then she saw them-----three men, dressed in warm robes and wearing crowns. And they all had woolly beards. A woolly beard would be a wonderful place in which to snuggle and keep warm. The men were carrying gifts and Addy listened to them talking. They said they would find a precious baby if they followed the bright star. Addy thought these men must be very wise, and she decided to quietly fly into the beard of Caspar and follow the star with them.

Addy could only measure distance in air miles, and she stayed in the beard to keep warm. The three men seemed to walk forever. It was a MAGIcal ride!

Can you find Addy?

Soon the men came to the spot where the star shone brightest. Addy was surprised to see other bugs, a kind she had never seen before. They had sparkly lights that twinkled as they flew. As Addy listened to the wise men talking, she learned they were called lightning bugs, and sometimes fireflies. Addy peeked out of the beard to look around. She saw shepherds with lambs as woolly as her warm beard, and they were all looking at a tiny baby in a bundle of straw.

The twinkling bugs hovered around the baby's head, flying in a perfect circle. Caspar told his friends this baby was called Jesus, and those little twinkly bugs were the bright lights telling the world that Jesus was divine. This is how halos came to be, and Addy was impressed with all she learned on her first nighttime journey.

She had become warm and toasty in Caspar's beard, and as she listened to the people talking about the wonderful birth of this baby, Addy decided to "fly with Jesus", and she followed him wherever he went. She frightened bad bugs away, and she protected Jesus, the flower of Christendom.

Today people say ladybugs are red because of the blood Jesus shed, and the black dots are reminders that bad things lurk all around us. Your mom and dad have read for years that three wise men came to the manger in Bethlehem. Now you know that one "smart little lady" came to see Jesus as well. And since that time, all of Addy's relatives have protected the beauty of God's creation.

I hope you find a ladybug in your garden!

The End